I'M STICKING WITH YOU

For Gabriel—who is brilliant in every way,
and whom I love unbearably much
—S. P-H.

This book is dedicated to chipped teacups everywhere
—S. S.

Henry Holt and Company, *Publishers since 1866*
Henry Holt® is a registered trademark of Macmillan Publishing Group, LLC
120 Broadway, New York, New York 10271 • mackids.com

Text copyright © 2020 by Smriti Prasadam-Halls
Illustrations copyright © 2020 by Steve Small
All rights reserved.

Library of Congress Cataloging-in-Publication Data is available
ISBN 978-1-250-61923-5

Our books may be purchased in bulk for promotional, educational, or business use.
Please contact your local bookseller or the Macmillan Corporate and Premium Sales Department at
(800) 221-7945 ext. 5442 or by email at MacmillanSpecialMarkets@macmillan.com.

Originally published in the United Kingdom in 2020 by Simon & Schuster UK Ltd.

First American edition, 2020
The artist drew and painted everything by hand in pencils and watercolor on
paper and composed in Photoshop to create the illustrations in this book.
Printed in China by Toppan Leefung Printing Ltd., Dongguan City, Guangdong Province

1 3 5 7 9 10 8 6 4 2

I'M STICKING WITH YOU

Smriti Prasadam-Halls
Illustrated by Steve Small

GODWINBOOKS

Henry Holt and Company
New York

Wherever you're going,
I'm going too.

Whatever you're doing,

I'm sticking with you.

Whether you're grumpy

or silly

or mad . . .

Through good times . . .

. . . and bad times,
happy or sad.

Whatever you're thinking, I am *all ears*.

I'm ready to listen to *all* your ideas.

CRACK!

Ready to be there to help you along . . .

Even if sometimes it goes a bit wrong.

ATCHOO!

Whatever you're doing,
that is the plan.

You may think I can't, but I bet you I can.

Because I will try things that I *never* would do.

Never, that is, until *you* showed me to!

Like peas in a pod,
you and I fit.

Like strawberries and cream,
we are a hit.

Whatever the game,
I'm on your side.

No mountain too tall,
no river too wide.

We sit by the cliff top.
We sit by the lake.
We sit by the ice cap.

I eat all the cake.

We—

Erm . . . Actually, Bear . . .
I think I need to be on my own.
If you don't mind?
It's getting a bit
crowded in here.

There's
bearly
any
room.

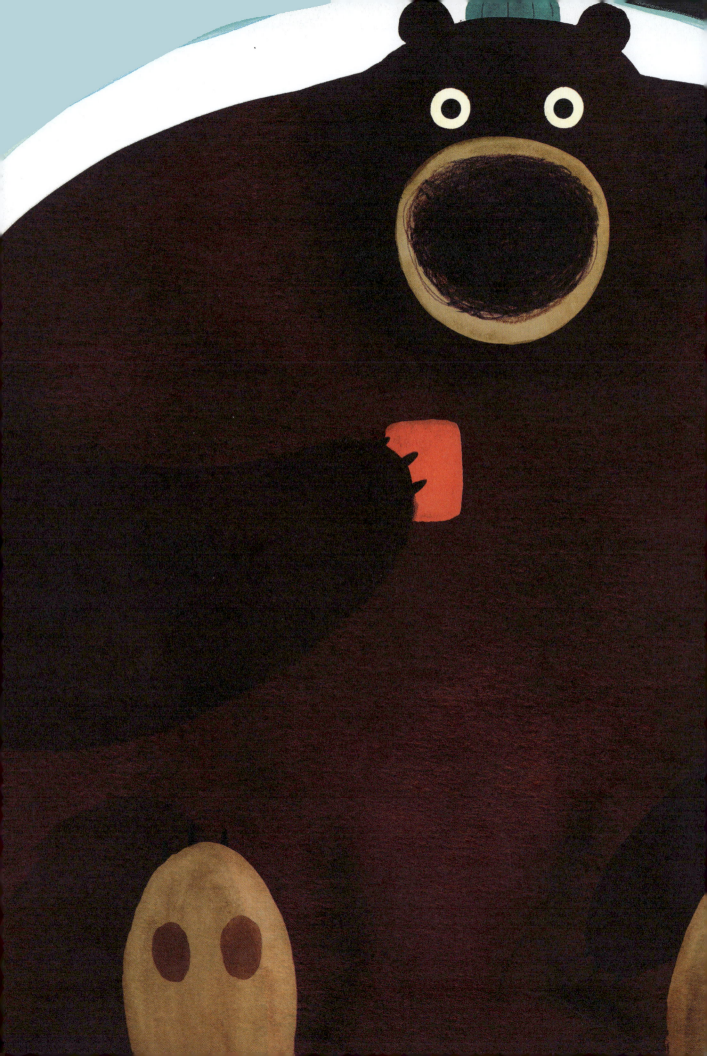

Really . . . ?
Are you *sure*?

Oh.
Okay then.

Ah! That feels better,
each thing in its place.

All neat and tidy—
there's so much
more space!

I can do what I fancy
whenever I wish.

Nothing's a squash
and nothing's a squish.

It's such a nice change to
do things alone . . .

Whatever I want to,
all on my own.

I've got all I need.
I don't have to share.

Everything's perfect,

except . . .

I MISS BEAR!

Actually . . .
Hey, Bear!
Bear

Bear

Bear

Come back!
Back

back

back

Who am I kidding?

Where would I even *be* without you?
Who else would listen?
What would I do?

Who helps me be the best I can be?
Who shares their very last chocolate with me?

Me without you?
It just doesn't work.

Me without you?
I'd just go berserk.

So like it or lump it,
you're stuck
with *me*.

For better or worse,
that's the way
it should be.

Whether we lose

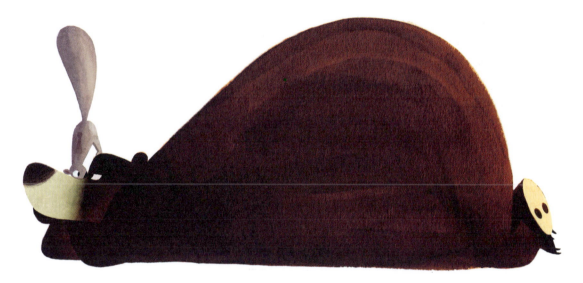

or whether we win,

we'll be there together
through thick and through thin.

We'll pick up the pieces,

We'll patch up the hole.

We'll mend what needs fixing,

Because that's how we roll.

When we're unstuck,

We won't fall apart.

**How could we ever?
We're joined at the heart.**

We'll fit back together
like bugs in a rug.

Like jam in a doughnut,

Like arms in a hug.

So . . .
**Wherever you're going,
I'm going too.**

Whatever you're doing,
I'm sticking like glue.

And whether you like it or love it or not,

We are a team . . .

And I LOVE YOU

A LOT!